Paradise Press, Inc

Exclusive distribution by Paradise Press, Inc.
© Creation, text and illustrations: A.M. Lefèvre, M. Loiseaux,
M. Nathan-Deiller, A. Van Gool
This 1999 edition produced by ADC International, Belgium
and published by Ottenheimer Publishers, Inc.,
Owings Mills, Maryland. All rights reserved.
SCO61MLKJIHGFEDCBA

Printed in Indonesia

Jungle Book

'''VAN GOOL'''

It was a hot evening in the Indian jungle and Father Wolf was waking after a long nap. He was feeling hungry and deciding where to hunt when a visitor arrived: it was Tabaqui the jackal.

"Beware Father Wolf! Shere Khan, the big tiger, has changed his hunting ground. He stalks his prey here. Protect your children!"

And with that the jackal rushed off into the dense jungle.

Shere Khan appeared a few minutes later. The wolf family defended their territory, but in their anger had not noticed the human baby that was crawling behind them.

"That baby is mine!" snarled the tiger.

"No! This is our hunting ground – go away!" growled Father Wolf.

Shere Khan sauntered away, planning to get revenge at another time for the meal he had just been denied. When he was gone, the wolves looked at the man-child.

"We should look after this child," said Mother Wolf. "We will call him Mowgli."

"First we must ask the opinion of the wolf council," said Father Wolf.

When Mowgli was brought before the council, Akela their chief asked, "Is it right that this man-child stays with us? Who here will protect him?"

An old bear, Baloo, was at the edge of the meeting, listening.

"I will teach Mowgli the law of the jungle, as I have taught your children," he suggested.

At the other side of the meeting the shadowy figure of Bagheera, the panther, was visible in the fading light.

"I will help Baloo to look after this child," she declared. And thus was Mowgli accepted by the wolf council and their people.

As the years passed Mowgli became strong and agile. The lessons from Baloo had taught him the ways of the jungle. He could swim and climb, he knew how to hunt to feed himself, and he knew the languages of all the animals around him. Mowgli was a good student.

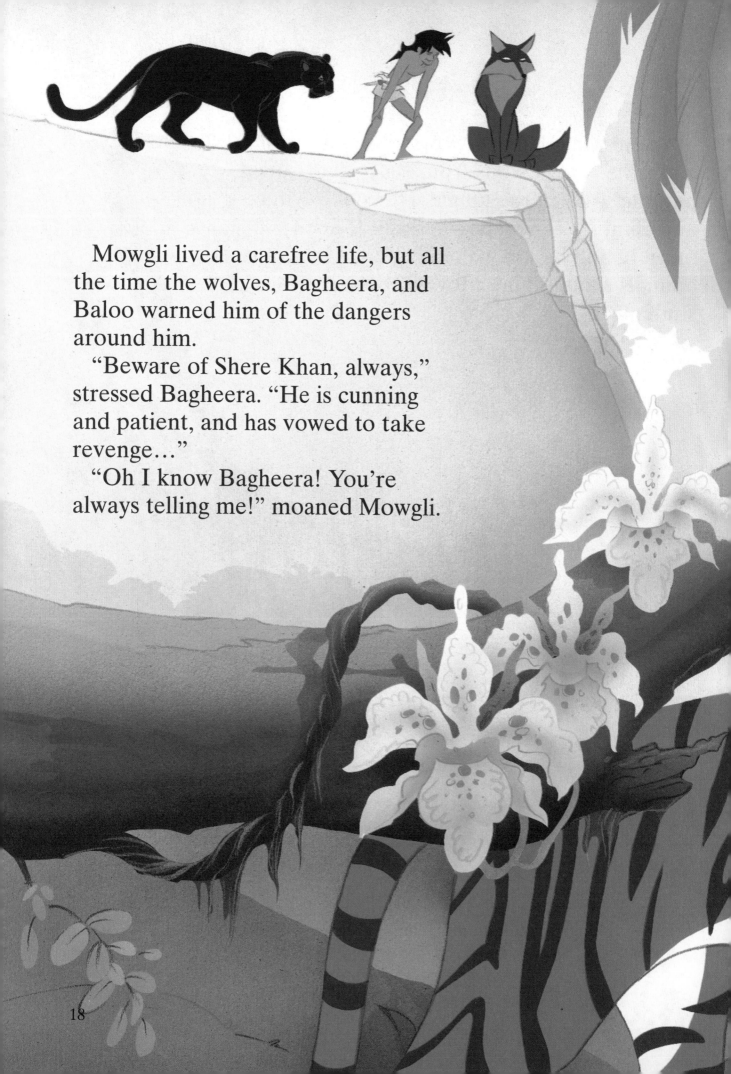

Mowgli lived a carefree life, but all the time the wolves, Bagheera, and Baloo warned him of the dangers around him.

"Beware of Shere Khan, always," stressed Bagheera. "He is cunning and patient, and has vowed to take revenge…"

"Oh I know Bagheera! You're always telling me!" moaned Mowgli.

Baloo warned him about
the monkeys. They had no
laws, unlike the wolves, and
loved to play tricks.

"Don't talk to them!" he
cautioned.

The monkeys, however, were very interested in Mowgli. One day, as he dozed between his two friends, he felt lots of small hands lifting him into the air. "Come and have fun with us, little man," they chimed, as they pulled him up into the tree.

When Baloo and Bagheera woke up, they could not find Mowgli anywhere and were worried. The monkeys must have kidnapped him!

"Let's go and see Kaa," suggested Bagheera. "He knows what goes on in the trees, and he does not like the monkeys."

Kaa was in his usual sunny spot and welcomed them to his lair.

"I can lead you to where the monkeys are living," he hissed. "Follow me."

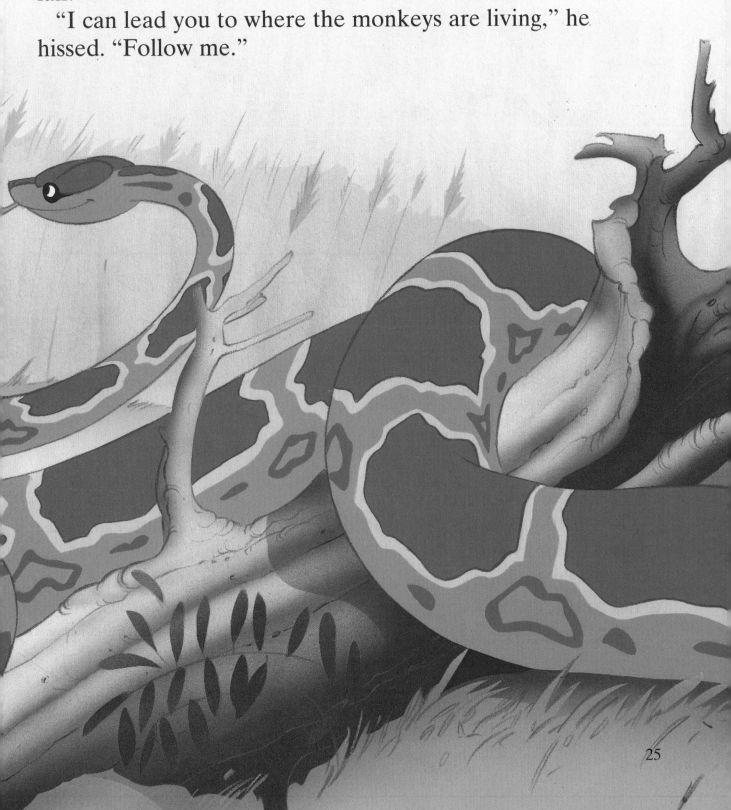

The monkeys had taken Mowgli to their hideaway, an old Indian town in ruins.

"Leave me alone!" wailed Mowgli as they pulled at his arms and legs, and tripped him up.

"No," cried the monkeys. "We're having fun!"

Suddenly there was a terrible roar and Bagheera was visible on the wall above them. Frantic, the monkeys threw Mowgli into a pit of snakes.

"I know your language," murmured Mowgli to the hissing mass, remembering his lessons from Baloo.

"We understand you and will not harm you," they replied.

A terrible fight broke out as Bagheera and Baloo tried to rescue Mowgli. There were too many monkeys for the two of them to fight. Baloo tossed them away, as they charged at him, but Bagheera was in trouble.

"Bagheera!" cried Mowgli. "Jump in to the water!"

The panther was relieved to hear Mowgli's voice above the screeching of the angry monkeys.

Suddenly Kaa uncoiled like a spring and pounced into the middle of the monkeys. To avoid him the monkeys jumped into an empty pit and were trapped.

"So this is young Mowgli," whispered Kaa when the fight had stopped. "He looks just like one of these monkeys."

"Thank you for rescuing me," said Mowgli politely.

"Now for my dinner," said Kaa. Hypnotized by the big snake, the monkeys were standing immobile in the pit. Bagheera and Baloo weren't feeling too well either... Mowgli took them home.

Then one night a few days later, the young wolves who admired Shere Khan for his strength, invited him to speak at their council.

"Mowgli, the wolves don't want you to stay anymore," he snarled. "You are a nuisance."

"Shere Khan, I'm not afraid of you!" cried Mowgli. "If my brothers want me to go then I will, but I will fight you first."

Mowgli decided to follow the advice of Bagheera after issuing the challenge to Shere Khan. He was going to steal fire from the human village. At the entrance of the village Mowgli saw a small boy carrying an earthenware pot full of ashes. Mowgli grabbed the pot and ran back to the jungle.

With a torch lit from the embers, Mowgli was able to successfully drive Shere Khan away. "He won't be gone for good, though," thought Mowgli, "and my brother wolves want me to leave. I am a danger to them more than ever now."

So Mowgli left his family of wolves and walked to the human village. He was hungry and dirty when he got there and could not understand the villagers. He looked like the wolves he had been living with and the villagers were afraid of his strange actions, and thought him mad.

Gradually though, the villagers grew used to Mowgli, and allowed him to tend their buffalo. He learned to speak their language, but thought their lives strange. He did not want to sleep in their houses. Mowgli still saw some of his friends; Grey Brother, a wolf, remained loyal and would visit with news about the jungle.

Mowgli wasn't unhappy living with the villagers, but he missed Baloo and Bagheera. He tried to adjust to their way of life, and to obey their laws. At nighttime they would gather to listen to the medicine man telling stories about the jungle, and Mowgli laughed at his ignorance. But there was one thing that frightened the villagers: Shere Khan.

One day when he met with Grey Brother, Mowgli asked his help to catch Shere Khan.

"Warn me when you know he is near."

"How will you catch him?" asked the wolf.

"I will use my buffalo…"

Not long after that meeting, Grey Brother came to warn Mowgli, "Shere Khan is sleeping nearby."

Together they herded the buffalo into the ravine, and surrounded the sleeping tiger. The buffalo, scenting the tiger, began to panic and before Shere Khan knew what was happening he was trampled by the buffalo. Mowgli sent the buffalo back to the village.

Mowgli set to work on the body of Shere Khan, and then rested the beautiful coat on a tree. The medicine man from the village came to see what Mowgli had done.

"You are only a shepherd, nobody will believe that you killed this mighty tiger. Give me the skin and I will show it to the village."

But Mowgli was suspicious of the medicine man. Grey Brother scared him away.

Mowgli was proud of what he had done; he had beaten his enemy with cunning and guile. He displayed the skin of Shere Khan to the villagers, but they threw stones at him.

"Get out!" they cried. "You're not human! Children don't kill tigers!"

Rejected by the humans, Mowgli returned to the jungle and displayed the skin of Shere Khan to the wolf council. His friends, Bagheera and Baloo, weren't surprised to see that he had succeeded. The young wolves were impressed, and they asked Mowgli to live among them again.

So again Mowgli lived and hunted
with Bagheera, Baloo and the wolves.
He had learned a lot living with the
humans, and had grown into a man,
but preferred life in the jungle with
his friends.